A WOODLAND MYSTERY™

The Diamond of Doom

A Woodland Mystery
By Irene Schultz

The Wright Group®

**To my well-remembered friend,
Gordon Anderson, with love**

The Diamond of Doom
©1996 Wright Group Publishing, Inc.
©1996 Story by Irene Schultz
Cover and cameo illustrations by Taylor Bruce
Interior illustrations by Meredith Yasui
Map illustration by Alicia Kramer

Woodland Mysteries™
© Wright Group Publishing, Inc.

The Woodland Mysteries were created by the
Wright Group development team.

All rights reserved. No part of this book may be reproduced
or transmitted in any form without written authorization
from the Wright Group permissions department.

The Wright Group
19201 120th Avenue NE
Bothell, WA 98011

Printed in the United States of America

10 9 8 7 6 5 4 3

ISBN: 0-7802-7228-5

What family solves mysteries...has adventures all over the world...and loves oatmeal cookies?

It's the Woodlanders!

Sammy Westburg (10 years old)
His sister Kathy Westburg (13)
His brother Bill Westburg (14)
His best friend Dave Briggs (16)
His best grown-up friend Mrs. Tandy
And Mop, their little dog!

The children all lost their parents, but with Mrs. Tandy have made their own family.

Why are they called the Woodlanders? Because they live in a big house in the Bluff Lake woods. On Woodland Street!

Together they find fun, mystery, and adventure. What are they up to now?

Read on!

Meet the Woodlanders!

Sammy Westburg
Sammy is a ten-year-old wonder! He's big for his fifth-grade class, and big-mouthed, too. He has wild hair and makes awful spider faces. Even so, you can't help liking him.

Bill Westburg
Bill, fourteen, is friendly and strong, and only one inch taller than his brother Sammy. He loves Sammy, but pokes him to make him be quiet! He's in junior high.

Kathy Westburg
Kathy, thirteen, is small, shy, and smart. She wants to be a doctor some day! She loves to be with Dave, and her brothers kid her about it. She's in junior high, too.

Dave Briggs

Dave, sixteen, is tall and blond. He can't walk, so he uses a wheelchair and drives a special car. He likes coaching high-school sports, solving mysteries, and reading. And Kathy!

Mrs. Tandy

Sometimes the kids call her Mrs. T. She's Becky Tandy, their tall, thin, caring friend. She's always ready for a new adventure, and for making cookies!

Mop

Mop is the family's little tan dog. Sometimes they have to leave him behind with friends. But he'd much rather be running after Sammy.

Table of Contents

Chapter 1:
Saturday Plans

It was Friday night.

No school for two days!

The five Woodlanders sat around the kitchen table making plans for Saturday.

Their little dog Mop lay under the table on Mrs. Tandy's feet.

Mrs. Tandy said, "Well, I like Bill's museum idea."

Ten-year-old Sammy waved a chicken bone in the air. He said, "Well, I like this chicken!

"Please pass me the chicken plate, and some muffins and plum jelly and ... "

His brother Bill, fourteen, said, "Hey, slow down, you pig. Leave a few bites for the rest of us."

Kathy, their thirteen-year-old sister, added, "And stop waving that chewed-on femur at us!" She said it like this: FEE-mer.

Sammy looked at the bone in his hand. "This is a femur? I thought it was a piece of chicken leg!"

Kathy said, "Femur is another name for it. If we do go to the museum

2

tomorrow, let's take it with us. Then we can look at it next to a dinosaur femur."

Dave Briggs, sixteen, sat at the table in his wheelchair.

He said, "I think we should go. I'll drive if we do."

Dave had a station wagon with hand brakes and a hand gas pedal.

Mrs. Tandy said, "Well, if we leave at noon we would get to the museum

3

around one o'clock.

"Then we could have lunch there before we start looking around."

Sammy took a giant bite of a corn muffin, and started talking with his mouth full. "Remember, I get first choice of what to see."

Bill said, "Why do YOU get first choice, King Sammy?"

Sammy said, "Because I'm the youngest, so you have to be nice to me."

Mrs. Tandy laughed. "Well, I'm the oldest, so you have to be nice to ME. And I get first choice."

Then Bill smiled. "Well, I'm the middle-est, so I get first choice."

Kathy added, "Well, I'm your only sister, so I do."

Dave said, "Here, guys. While you were fighting things out, I tore my napkin into strips. See, I rolled them up.

"Everybody take one from my hand. Whoever gets the longest piece chooses first, and so on."

They each picked a ball and opened it up.

Sammy said, "Hah! See! I was right. Mine is the longest. I get first choice, and I choose the mummies."

Kathy said, "Mine is second longest. I choose the life-sized cave family."

She added sadly, "I think the father looks a little like our dad looked."

Bill said, "Kathy, I'll choose the dinosaur room. Then you can check out that chicken leg bone."

Sammy jumped up from the table. He said, "No way! This is MY bone! I'm putting it in my pocket right now. I'll check it against the dinosaur myself!"

Mrs. Tandy said, "I'm fourth. I choose the insect and water animal displays."

Dave said, "And I'll take the rocks and the Jewel Room."

Kathy said, "This will be GREAT! I love going into the city! And the museum is like the whole world shown on three huge floors."

Bill said, "Too bad Mop can't go. He'd love it. He can't see that well, but he has a great nose. He could smell his way through."

Sammy said, "Boy, I bet he'd love a dinosaur bone to chew. Too bad these chicken bones make dogs choke."

They finished their dinner. Then they all cleaned up.

Dave said, "Hey, we should invite Chief Hemster to go tomorrow."

Bill said, "That's right! He went with us last time."

Sammy said, "Anyway, he'd want to come watch out for his girlfriend in the big city."

He smiled hard at Mrs. Tandy. He loved to tease her about the police chief of Bluff Lake.

Dave called the police station, but Chief Hemster said he was on duty all day Saturday.

But the chief added, "Call me before you start for home, though.

"I'll meet you halfway.

"I'd like to take you all out for pizza around six o'clock."

They thought that was a great idea.

Dave said, "We can call you around five."

.　　.　　.

They had no idea that at 5:00 on Saturday they would be prisoners.

Chapter 2:
The Mummy Room

"Hey!" Sammy said. "My shoes are stuck to this darn lunchroom floor.

"Does the museum ever get this basement floor washed?"

He lifted his foot. It made a noise like a piece of plastic cracking.

Bill and Kathy laughed.

Dave said, "Looks like they missed a few places with the mop."

Sammy said, "Well, they must have missed washing the part under my feet for about two years."

Bill said, "Come sit over here, Sammy. There's plenty of room."

But instead of moving next to Bill, Sammy sat right down on his brother's lap.

Bill cried, "Get OFF me, you big bag of beans!"

Then he pinched Sammy to make him move.

Sammy jumped up.

He asked, "Dave, did you see what he did to me?

"He pinched me. I sat on his lap to

keep him company and he pinched me.

"He's always such a pest."

Everyone laughed at that.

Dave pushed his wheelchair back from the table. "I guess we better get going.

"It's two o'clock already. This museum is so big, we couldn't see all of it even if we had a whole day."

Sammy said, "Right! On to the mummies."

Bill said, "It's weird. You hate sticky messes, but you like mummies.

"Most of them look rotten.

"All those dirty, yucky strips of cloth wrapped around. And the one without his wrappings!

"That poor little boy mummy with his cheeks caved in. And skinny legs and arms like brown bones."

Sammy said, "You wouldn't look so great yourself if you were thousands of years old."

11

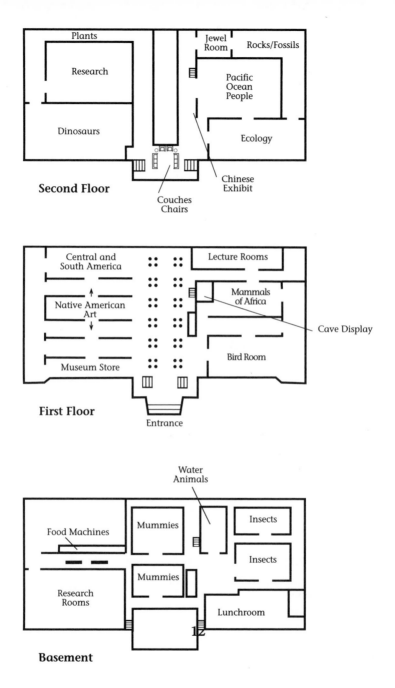

Second Floor

Plants

Research

Dinosaurs

Jewel Room

Rocks/Fossils

Pacific Ocean People

Ecology

Chinese Exhibit

Couches Chairs

First Floor

Central and South America

Native American Art

Museum Store

Lecture Rooms

Mammals of Africa

Cave Display

Bird Room

Entrance

Water Animals

Basement

Food Machines

Mummies

Insects

Insects

Mummies

Research Rooms

Lunchroom

For about twenty minutes they walked all around the huge mummy room.

Sammy said, "They look like rotting ghosts to me."

Kathy said, "I've seen X rays of mummies. You can tell what some of the people died from."

They moved on.

They stood in front of a wooden mummy box. It had a face painted on it where the mummy's face would be inside. Little people were painted all over the rest of it.

Dave said, "Boy, that sure is beautiful. And it's lasted more than two thousand years."

Kathy had been reading a card on the case.

Suddenly she said, "Listen to this! To keep the head of the dead king from rotting, the worker took the king's brain out,

13

through the nose."

Sammy said, "Yuck, Kathy!   That makes me sick!

"It's too bad Bill didn't live and die in old Egypt.   He doesn't have much of a brain.   He'd be a ready-made mummy."

Then he hit Bill on the arm.

Instead of hitting him back, Bill said, "Look over there, Sammy.   There's a whole case of tiny mummies."

Sammy hurried over to it.

He asked, "Hey, what ARE these little things?"

Dave said, "Believe it or not, they're animals. When a king died, his hawks and cats were killed and buried with him to keep him company. Sometimes even dogs."

Sammy said, "You're kidding. No one would kill a dog for that. No one's that mean."

He ran toward the door.

He said, "Dog mummies! I hate that! Let me out of here."

They followed him out and up to the first floor.

Dave said, "Kathy's turn for the cave family."

Kathy said, "Oh, good. I love that display. They look so ALIVE!"

Sammy said, "They sure do. The father dragging in a deer. And the mother holding the baby."

Kathy added, "And the two children

building the fire."

Bill said, "And the bigger ones skinning the animal."

Mrs. Tandy said, "I like that case, too. But it scares me a bit. I always expect them to come to life."

Sammy said, "Me, too. I always think I see them move a little."

Dave said, "I know what you mean. An eye ... or a finger. You even think you see them breathe, if you look long enough.

"We are almost there. The cave display is just around that corner."

But when they turned the corner, they got a big surprise.

Chapter 3:
The Cave People

They stood in front of the huge glass case.

Sammy said, "Holy cats! What happened here?"

Inside the case was a giant black cover, taped against the glass. It hid the whole cave scene.

Mrs. Tandy said, "Oh, dear. I was really looking forward to seeing it."

Dave said, "I wonder what's wrong. Do you think they're changing it? I sure hope not."

Bill said, "Let's find a guard. Maybe they'll have it fixed up later today."

He went to ask someone.

Sammy said, "Hey, look at that little door on the side of the case."

He walked over to it. The door was partly open.

Dave said, "Let's see, that door must lead to the back of the cave. You know, the part that looks almost like a tunnel."

Just then Sammy jumped back. The little door had opened farther, and it almost hit him.

Out came two men in museum workers' clothes.   One said to the other in a
rough voice, "I left the bug spray down
in the storeroom, Joe.   You go get it."

The man who spoke was tall and thin.

He had thick black hair ... and thick
black eyebrows that almost met at the top
of his nose.

And he looked mean.

Sammy wanted to ask the man about the cave display. But he was afraid to talk to him.

He looked around for Bill to back him up. But Bill was out of sight.

Finally he said, "Why is the cave covered? We wanted to see it."

The man said, "Well, it's closed for cleaning."

Sammy said, "How long will it take? We can come back later."

The man growled, "You're out of luck, kid. Forget it. Scram."

Sammy said, "You mean it's going to be closed until closing time?"

The man said, "That's right. I said forget it. Now run along, kid."

Sammy got mad!

He made his bull-dog face.

His hair stuck straight out from his head.

He said, "I'm not going to run along. Why should I? I have the right to stand here."

Kathy called, "Come on, Sammy. Let's get out of here."

Dave said, "Let's go. We can come back to the museum some other day and see the cave family."

Sammy said, "No, sir. It's a free country. I'm staying right in this hall. I'm not scared.

"There's a lot I can look at on the other side of this hall.

"There are the skulls of ten kinds of early humans.

"And all those stone tools."

Sammy looked straight at the black-haired man. He said, "I'm going to hang around this place for a long time. I'm never leaving!"

The man looked so mad, Mrs. Tandy

stepped over to him.

She said, "You have no right to tell us to scram! You were very rude. I'll report you to the front desk."

The man looked scared.

He said, "Oh, I'm sorry, ma'am. I didn't know you were with the kid."

In a friendly voice he said, "I was just afraid he might get hurt. We keep opening and closing this door. I meant no harm. Don't report me, please."

Mrs. Tandy said, "Then mind your manners next time you talk to visitors. Children or grown-ups."

The man said, "OK, ma'am, sure. I'll remember. There's my partner coming now. I've got to get inside."

He hurried halfway through the small doorway.

Sammy saw him fool around with the lock.

Then the man held the door open.

The other worker went through and he closed the door after them.

Just then Bill came up the hall. He

had a smile on his face.

He called, "Hey, guys! I had to go all the way to the other end. But I found a guard. He said the cave display will be ready right before closing time."

Kathy said, "That's funny. The man inside said it wouldn't be open all day.

"Anyway, let's head back down to the insects and water animals. Is that still your choice, Mrs. T.?"

She said, "It sure is. But it's Bill's turn to choose."

Bill said, "That's OK. The dinosaurs and the rocks and jewels are close to each other. We can do them together last."

Sammy said, "The furry spiders and the giant squid are waiting for us. Let's go!"

He ran in front of them. He called, "I'm going to be the first one there."

■   ■   ■

And he forgot all about telling them what he had seen the man do to the lock on the door.

Chapter 4:
Crawly Things

Back down to the basement they went.
Sammy led the way.
He said, "Here it is. Bug Town."
They went in. There were great big

cases, full of thousands of butterflies.

Kathy said, "Look at that bright blue one. It's my favorite."

Sammy made a face. "They may be sort of pretty, but bugs are bugs. They're still crawly."

Kathy said, "But Sammy, these aren't bugs. They're insects.

"Real bugs have a different kind of mouth, like these bedbugs over here."

Sammy gave a little scream. "Bedbugs!" He walked over for a look.

He said, "Yuck! Right next to them are stinkbugs! Great! Crawly AND stinky!"

Bill said, "Look at this display. It shows a moth head, bigger than life!"

Dave said, "Its feelers look like feathers."

Sammy walked into another room. Then he sneaked out into the hall to the candy machine.

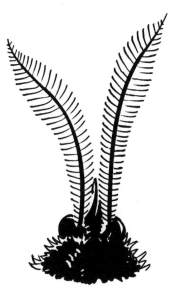

He put in money for four candy bars.

He ate two of them in one second, right there. One chocolate bar and one peanut-butter cup.

He put the other two into his back pocket.

Then he went back to the others.

Dave was saying, "Look at those claws on its head!" He was pointing to a beetle as long as his finger.

Bill said, "GIANT STAG BEETLE is what the sign says. How would you like to find that guy in your bed at night!"

Sammy said, "It says it's found in North America! Hey! That's here! I'm never going camping again!"

Bill laughed. "I'd protect you, Sammy. I'd get him off you with a flyswatter."

Sammy said, "A flyswatter! You'd need a baseball bat to get rid of that thing!"

Sammy began to scratch. He said, "I feel buggy. I'm itching all over. I'm going to wait in the hall."

He left the others in the insect room and stepped out. He ate his last two candy bars.

Sammy saw a machine with a sign that said MAKE A PLASTIC PIGGY BANK.

He fished out some coins. He dropped them into the machine. Wheels started moving inside. Two parts of a mold moved together. There were some funny noises.

The mold came apart. There stood a white plastic pig, as big as a fist!

It came falling through an opening in the machine.

Just then the rest of the Woodlanders came out into the hall.

Sammy showed them his piggy bank.

Bill said, "Not bad, Sammy. Here's some money to start you off." He reached into his pocket and took out all his change.

He gave it to Sammy.

Kathy and Dave gave him all that they found in their jeans and coat pockets.

Mrs. Tandy said, "Here, Sammy. I won't need my change, except for enough to call Chief Hemster."

31

Sammy put all the money into his piggy bank. It was more than half full!

Then he stuffed the piggy bank into his back pocket.

He said, "Thanks, guys! I'll never open it ... at least not until there's a real emergency. I bet there will be a million dollars in it by then!"

They walked down the hall.

Sammy said to Bill, "You go first."

Bill said, "Every time we come to this room you want me to go first. Why?"

Sammy said, "Well ... you know that giant squid hanging from wires near the ceiling?"

Bill said, "Of course. It's my favorite thing here."

Sammy said, "Well, I know it's dead. But what if somehow it came alive? I want you to make sure before we go in."

Bill said, "Some brother you are! You send ME in to be grabbed and eaten by a sixty-foot-long squid.

"I want all the money back I gave you."

Sammy said, "Nope. It's mine now. Besides, I was just kidding."

But he held Bill's hand as they walked in under the squid.

The room was filled with glass animals. Shiny sea worms. Big, bright snails. Giant clams. Even wet-looking seaweed, all made of glass.

Sammy said, "Hey, look at the sign near this giant clam!"

The clam was as big as a garbage can.

Dave read, "This animal is a danger to divers who step on it. The great shell closes so tight that it can hold on to divers' feet and drown them."

Kathy said, "Look at that beautiful snail next to it. The sign says it's full of poison."

Sammy said, "I love this room. But I sort of hate it, too. It's as crawly as the

34

insect room."

Dave looked at his watch. "Hey! We have to get going. We only have an hour till closing time."

So they rushed to the elevator to go up to see the dinosaurs.

∎　　∎　　∎

They didn't notice the man with thick black eyebrows following far behind them.

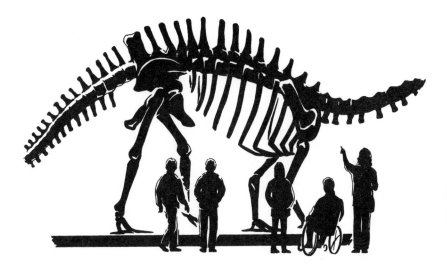

Chapter 5:
The Dinosaurs

The dinosaur hall was the biggest room
in the museum.

It had to be!

Right in the middle was the skeleton

of a dinosaur, ninety feet long and two stories high.

Kathy said, "It's bigger than our house!"

She pointed to its back leg bone. It was taller than she was. She said, "Now THAT'S a femur!"

Dave said, "Sammy, did you remember to bring your chicken bone?"

Sammy said, "Sure I did."

He started looking in his front pockets.

He took out a pocketknife.

Then he found a small rubber ball.

He had a bag of marbles. He said, "This is a new bag! Fifty marbles!"

He handed them to Dave. "Hold these, will you?"

Then he took out a ball of string, three paper clips, and two safety pins.

He said, "Never know when you might have to rig up a fish line."

Bill looked at the thick nylon string. He said, "You could catch a whale with that."

Sammy said, "Well, it's better than what you've got, which is nothing!"

By then Dave had a pile of things on his lap.

Then Sammy felt the four candy wrappers in his pocket. He pushed THEM down, fast!

Then he found a ball-point pen and a small flashlight.

Bill said, "Sammy, your pants must weigh twenty pounds. I'm surprised they don't fall down."

Sammy said, "Sometimes they almost do. Give me back my stuff, Dave. The chicken bone isn't in my front pockets."

He finally found it in his back pocket, under the piggy bank.

Dave said, "Look, this bone's smaller than the TOES of that dinosaur. But it's shaped just like the dinosaur femur."

Kathy said, "That's what's so interesting. Even human bones are a lot like this."

Dave said, "That sign says some full-grown dinosaurs were as big as ten elephants put together. But some were as little as rabbits."

Kathy pointed to a dinosaur on a painting marked PLANT EATERS.

She said, "Look at those leaf-shaped

plates sticking out of its back. It's called a Steg-o-saur-us. Its brain was only the size of a walnut."

Sammy said, "Now I know what Bill is! A Stegosaurus. Hi, walnut brain!"

Bill said, "Very funny, very funny."

Sammy walked over to a pair of the biggest dinosaur skeletons. One was biting the neck of the other.

He said, "That's me, fighting with Bill. I'm the one that's winning."

Bill said, "Then you're a Tyrannosaurus rex."

Sammy said, "What's a Ty-ran-no-saur-us rex?"

Dave said, "It means Tyrant King of the Lizards."

Sammy said, "What's a tyrant?"

Bill said, "It's a big bully, that's what! Like the one that's winning! Like you!"

Sammy said, "I'm not a bully. I'll get

you for that, Bill."

Bill said, "OK, OK, you're not. I think we've had enough of the dinosaurs. Let's just take a look at their eggs and go."

They walked over to the case with the eggs in it.

Sammy said, "I always think these eggs look like stone potatoes. How do they know they're dinosaur eggs and not just rocks?"

Kathy said, "From the shape. Plus, they were found near dinosaur footprints and bones.

"And they found lots of them together in a bunch, like a nest.

"Sometimes broken eggshells were found near an egg, all turned to stone.

"And now a scientist has found a fossil egg with the skeleton of an un-born baby dinosaur in it."

Sammy said, "A fossil LEG?"

Dave laughed. "Egg. She said a fossil EGG. Some fossils are animals or plants that have turned to stone. Some are millions of years old!"

Kathy said, "Or sometimes their shapes are marked in the stone ... where the plants or animals used to be."

Sammy said, "Are you guys making this up?"

Mrs. Tandy said, "No, that's true."

43

Sammy said, "Then I know what I'm going to be when I grow up, besides a police officer. And a clown. And a farmer. And a fire fighter.

"I'm going to be a fossil hunter!

"In fact, don't laugh, but I'm going to keep my eyes open for fossils when I'm digging in our yard!"

Dave said, "I'm not laughing. You can find fossils in lots of funny places. Down at the beach. In a driveway, even."

Bill said, "Come on, let's go see the Jewel Room."

They walked away.

■   ■   ■

And the mean-looking man kept tracking them.

Chapter 6:
The Jewel Room

They walked into the Jewel Room. It was in the back part of the second floor.

Kathy said, "Look at all those diamonds! All different tints."

Mrs. Tandy said, "My word! This takes my breath away!"

Sammy said, "Boy, it makes you want it all!"

Bill said, "And look at the size of this! It's called the Diamond of Doom. It's as big as a grapefruit!"

Dave read the sign near the diamond. "The first owner of this diamond DIED two months after buying it.

"The second owner died the day it became his.

"His family gave it to this museum so that no one could ever own it again.

"They believe that any person who owns it ... is doomed."

Sammy said, "That's not true, is it? Who cares though? It got the diamond for the museum! Even if it is the DIA-MOND OF ... DOOM!"

He made a scary face.

Then he said, "If I were a jewel thief, I'd go wild over this place."

Bill said, "You're wild without being a jewel thief."

Dave said, "Look at THIS diamond!"

Sammy went over to look. Dave was pointing at a big gray rock.

47

Sammy said, "That's no diamond."

Bill said, "That's one before it's been cut. They look just like plain stones when they're found."

Sammy said, "The sign says the diamond is the only gemstone made of one single thing, carbon. Hey, isn't carbon what coal is made of?"

Dave said, "Yep. When coal gets packed under tons and tons of rock it turns into diamonds."

Sammy said, "You're kidding! Well ... they should just get Bill to sit on a piece of it. That would turn it into diamond in a second."

Dave said, "Maybe instead I'll think of a new way to make diamonds someday."

Sammy said, "I know what I'm really going to be when I grow up.

"I mean besides a police officer.

"And a clown.

"And a farmer.

"And a fire fighter.

"And a fossil hunter.

"I'm going to be a guard in the Jewel Room. And save it from jewel thieves. And be a hero with my name in the papers!"

Mrs. Tandy said, "OK, hero. Let's go look at the gold bracelets and beads in that case."

Sammy said, "OK, but what's so great about gold?"

Mrs. Tandy said, "Well, for one thing, gold never rusts."

Dave was looking at a case near the Jewel Room door. Suddenly, he waved to Kathy to come over.

He whispered, "Sneak a peek out of this door, Kathy. Just walk by it, and look to the side. Isn't that the guy who was so mean to Sammy?"

Kathy walked across the doorway.

She took a quick look. She whispered, "You're right, Dave. He's just standing across the hall, watching this room."

Dave said, "I wonder why he's there. Well, don't tell Sammy. He'd probably run out and bite him."

Kathy said, "He gives me the creeps."

Dave said, "Me, too. Let's go back and join the others."

Bill was saying, "Last year in art shop I learned how to make a metal bowl. I hammered copper against a wooden shape.

"I bet they made these gold things the same way."

Sammy said, "That's the bowl you gave me, Bill. I keep my bubble-gum wrappers in it. I need six hundred to get a free cardboard checker set. I have forty-seven already."

Bill said, "By the time you get six hundred, you'll be a ninety-year-old man.

You'll be playing checkers with your great-grand children."

Just then a bell rang.

A voice came over a loudspeaker. "Closing time in fifteen minutes. All visitors must leave the museum."

The Woodlanders hurried to the elevator.

They got off on the first floor. They passed the cave display.

Dave said, "Hey! The cover is off. Let's stop to look. We still have twelve minutes."

Mrs. Tandy said, "My goodness! Look! They've added another cave figure!"

51

Kathy said, "You're right. He's lying under an animal skin at the very back of the cave."

Sammy said, "Let ME see." He ran in front of everyone to look.

All he could see was the animal skin and the top of a head of black hair.

Then the bell rang again.

"All visitors must leave the museum," the loudspeaker said once more.

They moved along.

Just then the guard Bill had talked to walked around a corner.

Bill said to him, "We saw the change in the cave display."

The guard said, "Oh, I didn't know it was different. What did they do to it?"

Bill began to explain.

But just then Sammy said, "Hey, there's the men's room. And I have to use it. And it's closing time. And I'm scared I'll get locked in the museum!"

Chapter 7:
Where's That Guard?

The guard laughed. He said, "Don't worry, son. We will wait for you to come out. We won't close the doors on you."

He walked to the front of the museum.

Sammy said, "It's spooky in the men's room."

Bill said, "I'll go in with you, Sammy."

Dave said, "Me, too. We have ten minutes. And the guard said he'd wait until we came out."

Bill said, "Look, Kathy, there's a restroom for you and Mrs. T. Meet you here outside!"

Once inside, Sammy said, "My stomach doesn't feel so good.

"I wish I hadn't eaten all those candy bars."

Bill said, "You little pig. How many did you eat?"

Sammy said, "Only four."

Dave said, "FOUR! No wonder you're feeling sick."

When they came out, Sammy hit Bill on the arm to thank him for waiting.

Bill hit him back this time. He said, "That's for sneaking candy bars without giving one to me."

Then the three boys joined Mrs. Tandy and Kathy in the hall.

They headed toward the front of the building. It was getting pretty dark inside the museum.

Kathy said, "I wish we didn't have to go home. We haven't seen half the things I wanted to see in here."

Dave said, "I know. We missed the moon rocks and the minerals."

Mrs. Tandy said, "And the Native American stone fish hooks ... "

Kathy said, "And the Bird Room."

They came to the animal halls.

All the big lights had been turned off. Only a few small ones were left on.

The sunlight was fading away. The tall windows were turning dark gray.

Sammy said, "Boy, it sure is dark in here near closing time." He moved over to Bill and held on to his arm.

They went past cases of stuffed wild animals from Africa.

Rhinos ready to charge.

Tigers chewing on a deer.

Hippos.

Elephants.

Kathy said, "With the lights so low, the animals look alive. See? Their eyes shine like real ones."

Sammy said, "It sure is quiet in here. I can't hear anyone but us."

Kathy said, "We must be the very last ones left in the museum, except for the guards."

Mrs. Tandy said, "I don't like this one bit. It's TOO quiet for my taste."

Bill was starting to worry. He pushed Dave's wheelchair a little faster.

They hurried along. At last they turned into the big center hall. They looked past the two huge stuffed elephants.

There was no one standing near the doors.

There was no one in the front booth.

There was no one anywhere.

Sammy wailed, "Where's that guard! He said he'd wait for us!"

Bill ran to one of the front doors. He tried to open it. It was locked.

Sammy, Mrs. Tandy, and Kathy ran up to him.

The four of them tried the other front doors. All eight were locked.

They walked slowly back to Dave.

Dave said, "Well, it looks like Kathy got her wish. We don't have to go home. In fact, we've GOT to stay here all night.

"We are locked in the museum until someone lets us out tomorrow morning!"

Chapter 8:
The Prisoners' Plan

Sammy shouted, "No way! I'm not staying here with all those mummies!

"There has to be a way out, and I'm
going to find it! Can't we break the

glass in a door and get out?"

Bill said, "Nope. This museum uses special glass."

Dave said, "Wait a minute, I have an idea. There's a pay phone at the front. We can call the police."

Mrs. Tandy said, "Wonderful idea. In fact, we were supposed to call Chief Hemster! Let's go!"

Bill said, "Look, there's the phone. But there's a sign on it."

Mrs. Tandy went over to read the sign. It said OUT OF ORDER.

Bill said, "Holy cats!"

Sammy said, "You mean rotten rats! Now what do we do?"

Dave said, "It looks like we really are prisoners here for the night. I guess we have to make the best of it."

Mrs. Tandy said, "Maybe we can at least find a place to sit down."

Bill said, "I bet we can even find someplace to sleep later.

"And we've got our coats with us. At least we won't freeze."

Sammy said, "But what will we eat? It's after five o'clock!"

Bill said, "Sammy! How can you even ask that? You just had awful stomach pains fifteen minutes ago. That's why we are in this mess!"

Sammy said, "What's that got to do with being hungry?"

Kathy said, "I'm a little hungry myself.

I guess we could eat candy bars."

Sammy screeched, "Candy bars! Don't say those words!"

Dave said, "Don't worry, Sammy. Didn't you see all those other food machines downstairs?"

Bill said, "That's right. At the end of the hall on the other side of the mummy rooms. They have corn chips and potato chips and popcorn."

Kathy added, "And I saw apples and sandwiches."

Mrs. Tandy said, "It seems to me there are machines for pop and milk and orange juice and coffee, too."

Bill said, "Why don't we go down there right now? At least it will kill time."

Sammy looked worried. He said, "Hey, Bill. Do you think those little lights will stay on? They won't turn

THEM off, will they?"

Bill said, "They probably leave some on inside all night."

Dave said, "Did anyone bring a flashlight besides Sammy's small one?"

No one had.

Dave said, "That's too bad. Well, we can get to the food machines, but let's go slowly."

Bill said, "Wait a minute! How about the elevators! Do they turn them off at night?"

Sammy said, "I'll check them out."

He ran about ten steps toward the back of the museum. In a second he was eye-to-eye with a bunch of stuffed tigers.

He shot back like a bullet and grabbed Bill's hand.

So all together they moved slowly back through the halls.

Now it was even darker.

The big tall windows were black.

Dave said, "If the elevators are turned off, you may have to leave me on this floor. The stairway is so long, I'd hate for you to have to carry me down."

Bill said, "If the elevators don't work, we are taking you down with us. We have to stick together."

But the elevator did work.

They all got on.

Sammy pressed the button.

The door began to close.

But Bill reached out and stopped it.

He stepped out. "I'd better walk down. What if we all get stuck in the elevator!

"Someone has to be outside. And someone strong has to be inside. You stay on the elevator, Sammy."

Kathy stepped out after Bill. She said, "I'm not letting you walk down in the dark alone."

So Mrs. Tandy pressed the DOWN button and the door closed.

Bill and Kathy walked over to the stairs.

They felt their way along slowly in the near dark.

When they finally made it down, the others were waiting.

Sammy said, "When we get near the mummies, don't let me look."

He closed his eyes hard, but he was peeking.

He saw the mummy-room doors.

Pushing Dave in front of him, he raced past them!

The others hurried after them to the food machines.

Sammy said, "Safe at last. We made it!"

Dave said, "Boy, am I hungry!"

Mrs. Tandy said, "I could eat a horse."

Bill said, "Well, you may have to. I just thought of something."

Dave said, "What?"

Bill said, "We don't have any money to use in the machines. All our change is in Sammy's piggy bank!"

Chapter 9:
What If It's a Mummy?

Sammy pulled his piggy bank out of his pocket slowly. He took a long look at it.

Then he kissed it on its nose.

He said, "I promised I wouldn't open

you until there was a real emergency. Well, here's the emergency! Good-bye, piggy!"

With that, Sammy hit the bank on the floor.

WHAM! It split open. The coins rolled in every direction.

Bill and Kathy ran around stepping on them.

Finally, they had them all picked up.

Then Kathy and Dave counted the money.

There was enough to buy five sandwiches and drinks.

There was enough left over to buy three bags of corn chips and three apples.

Mrs. Tandy opened her big purse. She took out five tissues.

She said, "Can't eat this fancy dinner without napkins."

Bill said, "You've got enough tissues in there for fifty people."

They sat down on the wooden benches near the machines.

Sammy took out his pocketknife. He said, "I'll cut up the apples."

When they all finished their apples, Sammy said, "You're not the only one ready for emergencies, Mrs. Tandy."

Bill said, "You mean because you had your knife?"

Sammy said, "No, I mean because after I used it last week to cut worms for fishing, I wiped it off on my pants."

Bill jumped up. "SAMMY! You mean we ate apples cut up with a WORM knife?"

Kathy said, "It's OK, Bill. In some

countries people eat worms all the time."

Bill said, "Well, NOT in THIS country! Sammy, that's disGUSTing!"

Sammy said, "All right, you brat. Next time we are locked up in a museum, I won't help you. You can stay hungry!"

After eating, they all went over to the drinking fountain.

The hall was almost black.

Sammy leaned down for a drink. He squirted water right into his nose.

He said, "I hate this. I'm starting to feel like one of those cave guys."

Mrs. Tandy said, "Imagine how different life was before the electric light was invented.

"This dim light is making me sleepy already. And it's early!"

Sammy said, "Well, I hate to imagine life before restrooms were invented. I have to go again."

So they all went with him over to the restrooms.

When they came out, Dave said, "I've been thinking. We might as well settle in for the night."

Kathy said, "But where? On the wooden benches?"

Dave said, "No, I've got a much better place in mind. Follow me."

Bill took hold of Dave's chair.

He said, "I'M taking you down the hall this time. I'm going to walk slowly, right past the mummy rooms.

"I don't get scared like SOME people."

That made Sammy mad. He poked Bill in the ribs and yelled, "BOO!"

Bill zoomed down the hall pushing Dave like a rocket!

Sammy came running along. He said, "Wow. You looked like the space shuttle going by. What happened to

71

your slow walk?"

Bill couldn't help laughing.

Dave pressed the elevator button.

The elevator came down from somewhere.

Kathy asked, "Where are we going?"

Dave said, "To the second floor. At the end of the Chinese exhibit there are three soft leather couches and three or four big chairs."

Bill said, "Kathy and I will take the stairs again, and meet you there."

Sure enough, there was the comfortable furniture.

Bill said, "Dave, you can take one couch. Mrs. T. can take another.

"Sammy and I will push these four big chairs together in pairs. Then they'll be as big as two more couches."

Kathy said, "I'll sleep on one set."

Sammy said, "I'll take the other. You

can have the third couch, Bill."

At last everybody was lying down.

Then Sammy said, "Hey, something's wrong. My chairs keep sliding apart, and I keep falling between them."

Bill and Kathy got up. They put Sammy's chairs together between two of the couches.

Kathy said, "Now they can't come apart."

Everybody lay down again. It was quiet for a minute or two.

Then suddenly Kathy said, "Oh my gosh." Her voice was shaky.

She whispered, "I think something else is wrong."

Dave said, "What, Kathy? Are your chairs coming apart, too?"

Kathy whispered, "Stop talking out loud."

Bill whispered back, "Why?"

Kathy got up. She went over to where Dave was. Bill, Mrs. Tandy, and Sammy got up and followed her.

Kathy said softly, "I was just thinking about when you were waiting to take the elevator up to this floor."

Sammy whispered, "What about it?"

Kathy said, "This. If we are in this building alone, why did you have to wait for the elevator to come down to the basement floor?"

Bill whispered, "You're right! Why wasn't it at the basement where we left it?"

Mrs. Tandy whispered, "How could it go up while we were eating? Unless ... "

Dave whispered, "Unless someone pressed a button upstairs."

Sammy whispered, "You ... you mean ... someone else is walking around this museum besides us?

"What are we going to do?

"What if it's a ... MUMMY?"

Chapter 10:
Sneaking Around

Bill whispered, "Should we try to hide? Or should we try to find him?   Or her? Or it?"

Dave said, "We can't hide all night."

Kathy was scared.

She whispered, "I don't want to just stay in one place, waiting for someone to get us."

Bill said, "Who could be here? Do you think someone else got locked in by mistake, like us?"

Mrs. Tandy said, "What if it's some poor person with no home? Maybe someone hid in the museum for a warm place to stay."

Sammy said, "What if it's a robber!

"Or someone who loves mummies!

"Or IS a mummy?"

Sammy's hair was sticking out like a porcupine's.

He whispered, "Let's go look. But one thing ... what do we do when we find this person?"

Mrs. Tandy whispered, "We should keep out of sight."

Bill whispered, "Right. We need to see him first. That way we would have a chance to decide what to do."

Dave whispered, "Where should we start?"

Kathy whispered, "We haven't heard any noises up here on the second floor. And we've been up here a pretty long time."

Dave whispered, "Well, let's go to the first floor, then, and start there."

Bill whispered, "I'm tired of whispering. Can't we just talk in low voices?"

Dave said, "Sure. Just keep the noise way down. And stay together, no matter what."

So to the first floor they went. They sneaked down the stairs, so no one would see the elevator light.

They lowered Dave in his chair, step by step, down the dark stairway.

Mrs. Tandy said, "This is sure a funny way to get to see the Native American art."

They turned into a huge display hall.

Sammy said, "What's that!" He grabbed hold of Bill.

There was a tall shape right near the door.

Bill said, "That's just a statue, Sammy. It's OK."

Dave said, "Let's sneak down along this side. Look all around those cases. He could be hiding behind any one of them."

Slowly, carefully, they all followed Dave. They made their way down one side of the nearly dark room.

When they got to the end they went back on the other side.

They found nothing.

Sammy said, "At this rate, it will take

us until next year to search the whole museum."

Kathy said, "What if we split up? We could go three and two together, and still stay all in one room."

Bill said, "Good idea. We can do the next room that way."

So Sammy, Dave, and Kathy went together. Bill and Mrs. Tandy went together. They all searched the next room.

They found nothing.

After they had gone through one whole side of the first floor, they came to a stop next to the African elephants.

They all sat down behind the huge wooden base.

Mrs. Tandy said, "John Hemster must be starting to worry about us. We were supposed to call him hours ago."

Sammy said, "He's probably worried that you found another boyfriend."

Dave said, "Well, I'm not so worried anymore. Maybe nobody else is in the museum after all.

"Maybe the elevator is set in some way we don't know about. Maybe if no one uses it for a while, the elevator goes up by itself."

Kathy said, "But what if someone IS here, Dave?"

Mrs. Tandy said, "We can't just stop looking."

Dave said, "You're right. I guess we have to keep going."

Sammy said, "Well, I'm tired.

"And I'm hungry again, too.

"And I wish I was back home.

"In our house in the woods.

"In Bluff Lake.

"With Moppy.

"In bed.

"With an oatmeal cookie."

Then Mrs. Tandy surprised them all. She said, "OK, I've been holding out on you. I baked these for our ride home."

She opened her purse.

She took out a big plastic bag of oatmeal cookies.

She said, "I'm still saving most of these for when we get out of here. But we each get two cookies now."

Sammy said, "Wow! Thanks! At least I get one of my wishes. Do you have

Mop in there, too, maybe?"

They laughed and ate their cookies.

Bill said, "I feel a lot better."

Kathy said, "Let's start looking again."

They searched the whole hall.

84

They looked in back of every case.

At last they came to a stop in front of the cave display.

Dave took a look.   Then he said, "Check it out!"

He was pointing into the back of the cave.

Sammy said, "What?   I don't see anything."

Dave said, "That's just it!

"The new sleeping caveman.

"The one they just put in today.

"It's not there!

"It's been stolen!"

Chapter 11:
The Missing Caveman

Sammy walked slowly over to the side door that led into the cave display.

He pulled on the handle.

The door came open.

Bill said, "Hey, Sammy. How did you do that without a key?"

Sammy said, "I just remembered something I saw."

He waved them over to him.

He said, "Look at this! You know that black-haired worker who was such a rat? Well, I saw him put a piece of tape over the side edge of this door.

"That little metal part that fits into the hole in the door frame can't come out. So the door didn't lock."

Kathy said, "Wait a minute. Do you think that guy stole the caveman figure?"

Mrs. Tandy said, "With all the other things in this museum, he stole the CAVEMAN FIGURE?"

Dave said, "That doesn't make sense! And why did he mess with the lock? A real museum worker would have a key to that case."

Kathy said, "And don't the workers have to check out at closing time? That caveman figure was big!

"They would have known he was carrying something out of here."

Bill said, "Wait a minute! What if he didn't really work here? What if he was just pretending to?

"What if he was a crook?

"What if he somehow found out what day they were going to clean the cave display, and turned up dressed like a worker.

"Maybe he could even fool the other museum people."

Dave said, "Still, why would he steal THAT? If I were a crook, that's the LAST thing I'd steal."

Mrs. Tandy said, "I'd go after the Jewel Room if I were a thief."

Dave said, "Just a second. Where

89

could you hide at closing time if you were
a thief? Where you might be in plain
sight, but no one would notice you?"

Bill said, "You mean ... in a display case?"

Sammy said, "Hey! You mean that guy hid in the case? He WAS the new caveman?"

Bill said, "That's right! Remember his thick black hair? Didn't that cave guy have the same kind of hair?"

Kathy said, "Oh my gosh! That guy was MEAN! I hope he's not the one sneaking around the museum.

"Dave and I saw him outside the Jewel Room when we were in there. He kept looking at us."

Sammy said, "I bet he was afraid Mrs. Tandy would report him."

Mrs. Tandy said, "I wish I had! Then maybe we wouldn't be in this fix!"

Kathy said, "What should we do next? What's he after?"

Mrs. Tandy said, "There are things

here worth TONS of money!

"There's the display of a Greek king's gold, three thousand years old. It's downstairs."

Bill said, "How about the gold from Egypt down there?"

Dave said, "And the display of bronze statues from Africa. A thief could get millions for those."

Sammy said, "All those things are down near the mummies. You guys are CRAZY if you think we are going down there again."

Dave said, "We have to give them a quick check. Then we can head up to the Jewel Room."

Sammy said, "I'm not going down there."

Bill said, "OK, Sammy. You wait up here alone."

In a second Sammy was wrapped

around Bill's arm. "I changed my mind! I'm going with you."

Kathy said, "I think we really would be safer if we all split up. That way if he surprises one of us, the others can come to the rescue."

Bill said, "OK, let's each search a room alone ... but keep meeting as we finish each set of rooms. Let's go down."

Then Bill took a look at Sammy.

Sammy looked terrible.

He looked scared to death.

Bill said, "I need some help. My sense of direction isn't too good. Can Sammy stay with me?"

All of a sudden Sammy looked much better.

He hit Bill hard, on his arm, and smiled.

He said, "Come on, Bill. Don't worry. I'll help you."

They carried Dave in his chair down the long steps.

Then, like ghosts, they silently searched all the rooms of the basement.

Chapter 12:
Setting the Trap

They found nothing.

Bill said, "That's it. The guy is on the second floor for sure."

Sammy said, "As long as there are no

mummies there, it's OK. Let's go up and catch that rat."

Dave said, "First, the bad news. You'll have to carry me up. We can't use that elevator, you know."

Sammy said, "No big deal ... I've been looking for something to build my muscles."

He waved his fists in the air. "Wait till you see me tackle that thief!"

He grabbed the handles on the back of Dave's chair.

Bill took hold of one wheel.

Mrs. Tandy and Kathy took the other.

Quietly, one step at a time, they carried Dave up the stairs.

They reached the second floor at last.

Bill said, "First let's search every room away from the Jewel Room. Maybe he's in one of them. We sure don't want him sneaking up in back of us.

"Meet back here in ten minutes. Then we can plan how to go to the Jewel Room together."

Sammy said, "What should we do if he grabs one of us?"

Mrs. Tandy said, "That probably won't happen. But if it does, YELL! Yell your head off!

"Then the others will know you're in trouble."

Then she said, "How about if you come with me now, Sammy? Bill, can you spare him?"

Sammy said, "Sure he can. He was just being nice to me before, because I'm so scared of mummies. But now I'll come with you and protect you."

Just a few minutes later Mrs. Tandy and Sammy came to a room full of rocks.

Mrs. Tandy said, "I think we've done something wrong. These rocks are near the Jewel Room."

Sammy said, "You're right. We aren't supposed to be at this part of the museum yet."

Mrs. Tandy said, "I think this door is the way back to the main hall. But you check the other one, down at the other end."

Quietly Sammy ran down the room and through the door.

The next thing he heard was Mrs. Tandy, YELLING HER HEAD OFF!

He turned fast to run and help her. But an arm grabbed him.

And a hand covered his mouth.

He heard Bill whisper, "Shh ... don't make a sound."

Then Bill's hand moved off his mouth.

Sammy whispered, "Let me go, you big jerk! I've got to help Mrs. T.!"

Bill said, "Everybody's here. Let's sneak up together and find out what's wrong."

So, next to Dave, they tip-toed through the room.

They heard voices in the next hall.

A man's rough voice said, "Don't move, lady, till I'm done tying your hands behind you. What are you doing here, anyway?"

Mrs. Tandy said, "I was in the restroom when the museum closed."

The man said, "Lucky for your brats

they weren't locked in, too. Or WERE THEY?"

Mrs. Tandy made up a story in a hurry. She said, "They left a little earlier for home. I was going to stay in the city. So they don't know I'm missing."

Then the man pushed her and said, "March. Through that open door to the Jewel Room.

"Good thing I came out for something, or I'd have missed you.

"As it is, I'm going to have to get rid of you, so you can't tell the police what I look like. Now GET MOVING!"

Kathy whispered, "He's going to hurt Mrs. Tandy!"

100

Dave whispered, "I know! We've got to do something, and fast!"

Bill said, "We've got to get him out of there so we can grab him."

Sammy said, "Getting him out is the easy part. All we have to do is make a little noise. But I bet he's got a gun. So how could we grab him?"

Bill said, "I know. Quick, give me your ball of string. I'll double it to make it even stronger. Then I'll tie it in front of the door, between those two cases.

"Let me have your knife, too, Sammy."

Dave said, "I get it. We make some noise, and he runs out and trips over the string."

Bill fastened the string to the leg of one case.

Kathy tied it to the other case.

Sammy was busy a little farther away from the Jewel Room door. The others were too busy to notice him. He was on his hands and knees.

Bill whispered, "Well, that's done. I sure hope that string is strong enough."

Dave said, "It has to be! It's all we've got."

Bill said, "OK, here goes. Move to the sides, behind these cases."

He waited until they were hidden. Then he threw Sammy's pocketknife against the wall.

It hit the wall, then rattled to the floor.

The man came running out of the Jewel Room.

Chapter 13:
Fifty Marbles

They could see a gun in his hand.

They watched in fear as his leg reached the string.

They saw him trip a little. With the

next three steps, he tried to keep from falling.

Then they heard things rolling all over the floor.

The man's legs flew up in the air.

The gun flew out of his hand.

It landed with a clang on the marble floor near Dave.

Dave leaned down and grabbed it.

The man landed flat on his back, hitting his head on the floor.

He was knocked out!

Bill ran over and sat down right on his chest. He held the man's arms against the floor.

Sammy sat down on the man's legs.

Bill said, "Our string almost didn't work. What did this guy slide on that threw him down?"

Sammy said, "Fifty marbles, that's what. I put them all over the floor while you were tying that string.

"I'm no good when it comes to mummies, but I sure know a thing or two about marbles."

Kathy ran into the Jewel Room.

There was Mrs. Tandy, lying on her stomach!

Kathy un-tied the rope from her hands. She rolled her over.

She said, "Oh, Mrs. T., are you all right? Oh, please be all right!"

Mrs. Tandy said, "I'm fine. I'm OK. I'm just so blasted mad!"

Kathy said, "But your knee is bleeding!"

Mrs. Tandy said, "It's just a little cut, Kathy. He pushed me down after he tied me up. The worst of it is that I've got blood on the knee of my best pants."

Then Bill called, "Will you two stop talking and bring us that rope! We can't sit on this guy all night!"

Sammy said, "If Bill doesn't get off his chest soon this guy is a dead duck!"

They tied the man up.

They pulled him behind a case ... so they wouldn't step on him when they picked up the marbles.

Then they went into the Jewel Room.

The cases were all open and empty.

There was a big bag on the floor.

Bill picked it up. He opened it and looked inside. Some of the jewels fell out.

All of a sudden, a voice called from the hall, "Stay right where you are!"

Sammy whispered, "Oh, great! TWO crooks! What a night to get locked in!"

The voice said, "Get your hands up in the air!"

Then another voice said, "Wait! They're all right. I know them."

It was the voice of Chief Hemster, coming up in back of the other man.

The Woodlanders yelled, "Hooray!"

The first man walked through the doorway. He said, "What in the world is going on here?"

Then Dave said, "Hey, wait a minute. You're the guard ... you said you would wait for us."

Sammy said, "Yeah. You forgot all about us. You guys locked us in."

The guard said, "Sorry about that. After I talked to you, I went to the main hall.

"I saw someone in a wheelchair head to the front door. A bunch of people were with him.

"I thought you had decided not to use the restroom after all.

"Then, tonight, when I got home, I began thinking.

"Something was wrong. I remembered the people I saw were all adults. With someone else in a wheelchair.

"I realized you might still be in the museum, so I came back."

Mrs. Tandy said, "Well, how did YOU turn up, John Hemster?"

Chief Hemster said, "I started to worry when I didn't hear from you.

"Finally, I went to your house with the key you gave me.

"There was poor little Mop. He was hungry, so I fed him.

"I knew you had never gotten home.

"Finally, I put him in my police car and drove down here.

"But what are those jewels doing on the floor?

"Why are they out of their cases?

"And how did you end up with them?"

Dave said, "Here, you take charge of this."

He handed Chief Hemster the gun.

Bill said, "Look outside near the case on the right. Then you'll see why these jewels are all out."

The guard stepped out of the Jewel Room door. He shined his light around and saw the man, all tied up.

He yelled, "Jumping catfish! Who's this?"

Mrs. Tandy said, "He was hiding in the museum. He caught me and threw me down. The kids saved me!"

Sammy said, "Uh-huh. And because of him, I'm missing fourteen marbles!

"But at least we caught him. That's what he gets for messing with the Diamond of Doom!"

Then Bill told the guard and Chief Hemster about Sammy's marbles.

The guard said, "My boy, don't worry about those marbles.

"We will gladly get new ones for you.

"Fifty marbles!

"A hundred marbles!

"A thousand marbles!"

He turned to Mrs. Tandy. He said, "And you. Let me help you to a seat.

"Roll up your pant leg so we can give that knee some first aid."

Chief Hemster said, "Don't bother. I can do that."

Sammy began jumping around saying, "Mrs. T.'s got two boyfriends."

Mrs. Tandy said, "OK, Sammy. I see I'll have to do something to shut you up."

She took a cookie out of her bag. She popped it into his mouth.

The guard called the city police.

They took the jewel thief away.

A reporter walked in.

A crew from a TV station turned up.

They filmed everybody for the ten o'clock news.

They even got Sammy to pose with his marbles.

At last the Woodlanders went out to the car with Chief Hemster. Mop jumped all over them and licked their faces.

Four hours late, they drove to the pizza place for dinner. They had ice cream, too.

Then they ate cookies all the way home.

And Sammy said, "This is the best Saturday I've ever spent at the museum.

"We saw everything. We caught a thief. We are going to be on TV. We are heroes!

"So listen, let's start making plans. Where should we go NEXT Saturday?"